LYDIA THRIPPE!

Daniel Sloate

Lydia Thrippe!

A Critic's Diary
Followed by *The Lydiad*

Guernica
Toronto·Buffalo·Lancaster (U.K.)
1999

Guernica Editions Inc. acknowledges the support of the Canada
Council for the Arts for its publishing program.

Guernica Editions Inc. also acknowledges the financial support of
the Government of Canada through the Book Publishing Industry
Development Program (BPIDP) for its publishing activities.

Antonio D'Alfonso, Editor.
Guernica Editions Inc.
P.O. Box 117, Station P, Toronto (ON), Canada M5S 2S6
2250 Military Rd., Tonawanda, N. Y. 14150-6000 U.S.A.
Gazelle, Falcon House, Queen Square, Lancaster LA1 1RN U.K.

Legal Deposit — Second Quarter
National Library of Canada
Library of Congress Catalog Card Number: 98-73308

Canadian Cataloguing in Publication Data
Sloate, Daniel
Lydia Thrippe : a critic's diary followed by The Lydiad
(Prose series ; 53)
ISBN 1-55071-073-7
I. Title. II Series.
PS8537.L55L93 1999 C813'.54 C98-900807-X
PR9199.3.S55124L93 1999

Foreword

The following excerpts were assembled very carefully by one of Lydia Thrippe's oldest and greyest admirers, Dr. Sloate. The latter met Lydia some fifty-odd years ago at a box luncheon which they had both crashed. The chemistry between them was subtle and pervasive. They have seldom lost touch with each other in space or time, mutually fecundating each other.

Dr. Sloate was responsible for the light of day given to Lydia's early texts, published in *Brèches* in 1977. An admiring bog acclaimed them, even to the fens in Boston. Since then, Lydia has been busy with charitable works which are not publishable, and especially with nivaponics which she learned from Mrs. Waning.

In her Diary, Lydia plunges us into the thick of things without necessarily identifying her friends and enemies for the hapless reader. Perhaps a word could be said here about the personages that flit through these pages in order of appearance:

The Glyptic (Miss Fake Glyptic): Lydia's arch enemy. An academic and proud of it but who is not above the occasional *canular*, preferably at Lydia's expense.

Lord Oxthorpe (Old Oxe): distinguished connoisseur of lutes and boy lute players. Known for his vast knowledge of sexual kinks and his understanding of deviant minorities.

Tanya Scève: an inept medium, but whose pithy epigrams are often quoted by Lydia. Husband's death unlocked the doors of the hereafter, apparently.

Gillespie (various unkind epithets are used with this person): the mystery of Gillespie's gender is a running gag throughout the Diary until Old Oxe elucidates it.

Rod Coverley: interested (perhaps) erotically in Lydia, although this is never made clear to anyone, especially Lydia. Unstable.

L.L. Spurge: the infamous one who so viciously attacked Lydia on every front in *The Lydiad*. Often gratuitous in his aggressiveness, he is nevertheless a brilliant scholar whose definitive works on Leibniz and Diderot leave nothing to be desired, except, in Lydia's view at any rate, their long-overdue participation in an *auto da fé*. The rivalry between Lydia and him is often petty in the extreme (and in this they are true dwellers in the Groves) but it is always a slice of life in the crawler lane.

Velva Rose: other than her "nice name," Velva has few distinguishing characteristics. She is a close friend of Lydia's. Unstable.

Mr. Toon: husband to the above; a pastry cook. Stable.

Lillian: brother to Lydia who insists on wearing her clothes in public and private. Likes leather and aviators. No respect for the plight Lydia finds herself in because of his antics, nor does he respect the sanctity of her documentation closet wherein he takes refuge all too often. Unstable.

Olive O.: attractive to men; often is a member of a bevy.

Frau McCarthy: another medium, perhaps a witch. Keeps chickens that may not be what they appear.

Professor Silvio Bung: academic who struts briefly on Lydia's stage and then is heard no more, a victim of black magic.

The Toad: not a personage of course, but an important periodical where Lydia publishes her brilliant articles.

Mrs. Waning: not one of Lydia's favourite persons. She is a specialist in nivaponics (see entry on her winter garden at Gigglehook) and in the Groves is a well-known Trollope woman.

Dom Paddy: not one of Lydia's favourite persons. Expert in arcane psychoanalytical theory, in scabrous verses and Krafft-Ebing.

Marjorie Kelp: not one of Lydia's favorite persons. An "artscrafter" who mounts seaweed in glue.

Minerva Mount: usually merits the epithet "vulgar" whenever Lydia mentions her name. Loose in morals with a tribatic penchant.

Reverend Wasperd de Winter: enigmatic and heteroclite. Plays a role of no consequence in Lydia's life. Connection to Mrs. Waning remains obscure even though everything that could be probed, was probed, and then some.

Herr Klapp: neighbour of Lydia's whose obsession with order takes odd turns whenever Lydia is watching.

Là-Là: Lydia's niece, born in Quebec. Likes to tease her aunt but usually manages to disgust the latter.

A Critic's Diary

Such waste! Attended a lecture on those old *tumuli* things, given by Miss Fake Glyptic herself who seems to have set herself up as Miss Expert on Historical Erections (on vases only of course — Etruscan especially) with the occasional titillation of alfresco wall orgies but not one nod of her head in the direction of the Comic Muse. Such a painful creature, and as I say, the whole tedious time was ill-spent as I had intended to get into Lord Oxthorpe's new book on boy lute players. Skimmed through the footnotes on Fri. last and noticed his omission of Bach's mistake in gender on one of his scores ("pour *la* luth"). So juicy; how could Oxthorpe have resisted? Too facile, I suppose he'd say, but still the thrill never dims whenever I think the Old Wigged One believed that "lute" was feminine in French! I'm going to check in the book-body next Fri. and if Oxthorpe doesn't mention it at all, I'll have to write. We can't let them all dry up on us. It turns asphodel into sand, as poor Tanya Scève would say. Besides, a critic has to get her own genders straight and see to it that others follow the proper dots.

Saw Gillespie (first name? last? soubriquet?) as I left lecture. Speaking of genders, I have never been able to determine with any certainty whether Gillespie uses square brackets or crescents. Anyway, IT spoke to me just as the exiting crush of the melancholy few who had been exposed to Miss Fake's lecture was at its peak. IT asked me a question about "beats" I think — was IT speaking English? — and when I didn't answer, IT rasped out something about going to the "boozery" and was I interested in accompanying IT. (Remember to delete the preceding.)

Rod was there but I did not verify this. I know why Miss Fake Glyptic invited him though (if he *was* there): his Etruscan nose. I remember noticing his nose for the first time during a talk on "ultimates" we both attended a few years back: he was sitting three rows ahead of me, with his head turned just so and his profile showing. A show-stopper! Even the Glyptic stopped breathing, but can one always tell? Anyway, Rod was smiling a lot, in that sideways fashion he has perfected, and was nodding and becking to everyone's delight. I'm not sure of what I'm about to state but I believe the Glyptic and Rod were arm in arm after the lecture, but I do doubt. I must admit I was too fascinated by Gillespie's atrocious footwear to notice much else. But somehow I was at peace; that lovely Etruscan profile was etched in my mind and I was anxious to get home and kettle up. Off.

December 3

L.L. (he of the basket case brain) was odious as usual the other evening. Luckily there is the life of quiet dignity the spirit affords. I presume L.L. has a life of the spirit but surely he doesn't shake it well before using . . . At table I was reminded of a spicy [*illegible*] about Thaliarchus and was on the point of recounting that amusing anecdote which always sets the table at merry odds — although humour drawn from the classics can fail — when L.L. grossly interrupted to quote a few lines from Horace. He said them quickly so solecisms might not be spotted, but I laughed when he had finished to show the others that I had detected what they had not, even if it wasn't there (or *was*). L.L. looked down his nose at me (that nose told by an idiot, I add) but he went on about *gonads*, I believe. Anyway, Leibniz was mauled for a good twenty minutes; I was so fed up with all the thick-lipped mumbling that I rose. I proposed a toast to Thaliarchus but I noticed no one joined in except of course L.L. and just to be smart he poured his glass all over my shoes claiming it was an old Tartar custom. So bo-ring. Off.

December 3

L.L., like the incurable assaholic he is, was spouting some half-baked Leibniz drivel last night in a Portuguese restaurant we all just happened to be in, and that no one understood let alone listened to. When asked to pass the butter I passed *wind* instead but he did not take the hint,

just blunderbussed on, quoting something from Re-
marque (or was it Rilke? One of that leather-booted
bunch anyway), and actually claimed to have found a
link and/or links between Horace, Thaliarchus, Leibniz
and the Third Reich. I was tipsy by then, tipped over a
glass on L.L.'s lap in the best Tartar tradition, called him
a name that made a few faces burn (can't remember
what it was now, but it involved labial palps) and then I
was carried out in some dignity to the men's room — I
had actually given orders to this effect beforehand,
knowing L.L. would be crouched in the ladies' room to
finish me off. He was foiled by the oldest ruse in the
book but obviously it was too subtle for his melancholy
assaholic brain to grasp. That is the word for him: Old
Melanie or Old Thanatosis Puss. What a bore! Just before I passed out, I saw him buttonholing a cheap imita-
tion of the Venus de Milo, braless and inscrutable near
the Coke machine. Off.

December 3

I do miss Velva. I remember the twinge between my legs
when I first heard her name: Velva Rose. Soft and moist
with a little fuzz thrown in. Dear Velva. I wonder what
her obsession with flatcars means . . . The last one she
acquired took up most of the living room. True, Old
Oxe once had a thousand-pipe organ in his bedroom
before he became interested in boy lute players, but
really . . . The imponderables! I mean who would ever
have thought of a flatcar as décor except soft Velva

Rose? And the lovely *mole* on her tongue! At least that is her impish explanation for her cleft. Over the years of speech, the rough edges have softened and she has got it down now to a discreet lisp. Anyway, am to have tea and dumplings with her if that idiotic pastry cook husband of hers gets off his sponge cake buttocks long enough to make them. I'm so glad Velva kept her maiden name and did not take his. Imagine: Velva *Toon*. Grotesque.

December 3

I simply do not notice the time passing although the calendar seems stuck for some reason. The White Queen would know, or Velva who has a thing about dates, or Rod Coverley. Speaking of whom: I have the most vivid memory of him that rainy day a month or so ago when he bumped into me on the street and scattered some photos I was carrying all over the place. Not only did my photos start dissolving in the rain but Rod's fly as well . . . He explained that in deference to the worthy combat against pollution, he had bought a pressed paper suit, and was a living example (nearly naked by now) of the horrors of acid rain on people. I think he meant this as an apology, the darling. Unfortunately the rain stopped and so did all that lovely dissolving. Must call him soon and tell him I saw a second-hand compressor going for a song. He collects them. I suppose I could have sent it along as a gift but I was afraid the colour might jar with his interior. Off.

December 3

The date is peculiar. It was the third yesterday I'm sure, but then calendars are intrinsically monotonous . . . Cornered L.L. the other day — when was it? One of these thirds — asked him to tell us how Leibniz met his maker. He flatly refused, saying it was too macabre and not in fashion anymore. I knew, however, that he could be drawn out and let his fool hang loose if I baited him properly. So I rejoined (all this over dumplings and tea at Velva's some third or other) that tradition would have it Leibniz died while *stuffing a hen with snow*. He rose immediately to the bait (and to his feet), turned a tortured magenta, then through clenched teeth spat out: "Thrippe, you lie. One, you know full well it was Bacon; two, it was a cock." Isn't that precious? But it worked: he turned towards Velva and told her that Leibniz had never really died at all because we in this room were still talking about him over tea and dumplings and that his spirit was present, etc., etc., but that physically he had smothered on a shoe in a fit of rage over an earthquake. Naturally he was baiting me this time but I nodded my assent and his pink edged bluewards. I let him dangle there. Velva was splendid, merely lisping innocently, "*His* shoe?" I won't record the rest because my face hurts.

December 3

I often compare my daily entries here to Alain's *Propos*. They are a genre unto themselves: just the right tone, decorous and sweet; just the right length, a page or two, with some "detached leaves" for the usual reasons. And lastly of course is the Eye, the Depth, the Breadth of Insight. Rod would call it "Extension," the dear boy, but he does have a brain as well. Where I bifurcate in terms of Alain is in not setting pompous topics for myself to discourse on like Life, Death, Infernal Machines, etc. Oh, they are all there of course, but they are approached with a subtle grace that the Old French Fart lacked to an appalling extent. Oh dear, there's Rod again. Knocking at my door I mean.

Afterthought: Should I wear the hair in a concave bun or leave it hanging? Can't think linearly when Rod's at hand.

After afterthought: Oh, the spirit of the stairs I seem to have today! Just received a letter from a young poet in Ontario asking my permission to use my name in a Gay Arbor Day ceremony. The capacity was not mentioned. I don't think I should answer. It might be a trap set by L.L.Spurge himself.

After Rod: *Bliss is a state, after all* (my italics). Off.

December 3

I do worry about Lillian and my pantyhose and garter belt which he is wearing somewhere about town at this very instant. What if he should forget he has them on and get crushed in an accident? What about doctors and nurses? They would contact me, I suppose. Could I deny he is my brother without hearing the cock crow thrice? Possibly not. But even on a slab in the morgue, think of it, with my favourite garters and all. You simply cannot talk the man out of it either, as Velva Rose and I have tried to do God knows how many times. He refuses to listen to reason, just lady-squats on the nearest toilet seat and sings at the top of his lungs, "I'll never smile again" which he finds uproarious — so does Velva actually, but I draw the line. I can't keep on hiding my clothes from him forever. I have to wear them in public places. He does not. But he *does*. Would he were locked in that closet inside of which he should have remained closed until my death!

Ultimately, it's selfishness that's smeared all over his eyes, not mascara at all. I don't know if he has had any therapy — or surgery for that matter — although he once invited me to feel, which naturally I [*illegible*] . . . However, a sister is a sister is a sister as Velva keeps telling me, poking a finger through an antimacassar annoyingly as she makes her point a trifle too pointedly as usual. But then Velva dear has redeeming charms: no intellect; no shape; no wit; but such a nice name! And her pastry cook hub *does* dote on her. I have no one but Lillian when the chips are down, I suppose. And Rod? No. Away with illusions. I must muster my courage and tell Rod to fuck firmly off.

Afterthought: Lillian should be wearing tights instead of pantyhose in terms of his depressed ass.

After afterthought: This entry to be published with the *Detached Leaves* after my death.

December 3

I'm positive Rod has poems in his drawers. If only he'd submit them to me, the tender shy puss, I'd get Oxthorpe on them. Old Oxe loves young poets (the younger the better, especially if they play the lute); he has such a discerning eye (the good one, under the patch) when he isn't dozing. There was an evening that comes to mind — it happened about a year ago at the Glyptic's when we were still on speaking terms — when Oxe fell asleep as usual after cognac. His cigar went out the minute he closed his eye; it no doubt was his way of shutting out the Glyptic's discourse on (again) "ultimates": this time she was being hysterical about spheres, from Lascaux bulls to Tenian objects to Balthus; suddenly L.L. turned to Olive O. on his right and in a very loud voice said, "Or the Ball, from cavemen to faggots." It was one of the few times I have felt anything but vomit for the man . . . Well, the Glyptic (who of course has never received the benediction of the Comic Muse) asked Spurge to leave. He said no. She said you must. He said no. She said at once. He said no. And so on like tots fighting over a sandpail. It was then that Old Oxe struggled awake, and as his cigar burst into flame he boomed, "What was that about spherical balls?" Naturally the Glyptic was flustered, and making a pitiful attempt to play the hostess, weakly asked the Spurge to continue. He said no. She said you must. He said the whole idea had been hers and that the ball was in her court. So Miss Fake herself lurched into the most arid talk on eroticism I have ever heard. Even her tiresome Etruscan phase had references to blood rushing to the occasional organ, but this! After a few flaccid moments, Old Oxe was fast asleep once more, and L.L. was pinching Olive O. where it doesn't hurt, and I tipped over several quasi-full cognac glasses quite, but *quite* deliberately. Shambles ensued. Someone struck someone, but here my recollection is not dependable and therefore will not be recorded. Suffice it to say the Glyptic's party was a great success, *malgré elle*. And Old Oxe spent the night in his armchair since no one could remove the cigar from his mouth. Off.

December 3

There is to be an open air party tomorrow at the Botanical Gardens. I may attend. The one last year was uproarious, although taste was crucified. We all have to let the bun down once in a while, and these popular gatherings are perfect valves — not your cotillion of course — but one is so deliciously anonymous. I intend to keep a record of the whole thing this time. In hospital last year with a *tabula rasa* afterwards and could not remember the tiniest tad.

Saw Frau McCarthy this morning as she was feeding her chickens. She has a heated balcony and keeps chickens in there summer and winter. We all signed a petition but the birds remained where they were. Apparently her grandmother is the mayor's mistress (this from dear wag Velva); I know something is odd about her birds but I cannot put my finger on it for the life of me. I watched her for a good ten minutes spoon-feeding them until she noticed me staring. I moved away quickly since she does have something of a reputation as a witch. This is another delicious panel of my mind: the obscure corner where the light of Reason simply balks. I enjoy it. I intend to see poor Tanya Scève about this very soon. She, after all, watched her husband die on a toilet seat and it wrenched her spirit so that she has been psychic ever since. I think I'll tell her about Lillian as well; maybe he is simply a figment as I have not seen him for weeks, nor have any of my *unmentionables* disappeared lately. I think Lillian is an appropriate subject for a séance; certainly more fascinating than the usual knocks, wails and effluvia. I wonder if Frau McCarthy's chickens are real? I wonder if the Frau herself is real? Am I real? But I play for the gallery. Off.

December 3

Rod Coverley was at the Botanical Garden Party. It began to snow, so we all had to move inside to the shelter of the palm trees. It added a lark-like note to the proceedings. The Glyptic was wearing a flower mask that was tasteless in the extreme but it did match her poncho perfectly. Lord Oxthorpe didn't make it to the palms and may still be standing outside as I write this; I had whispered a good word to him about Rod's drawers full of poetry and he instantly made a movement which, unfortunately, was arrested in mid-shuffle by the snow. Poor Rod! He was too shy to help Old Oxe inside, preferring instead to get undressed near a public radiator. Tarts were served, and ices (actually "snow cones," as Velva remarked), and a preposterous hogshead of fake sack. This inane touch of the past was Olive O.'s idea, egregious in the best of weathers but when both Celsius and Fahrenheit agree as they did at the time, the sack froze and had to be sucked . . . I stuck to the tarts (slightly fermented I swear) and was enjoying the music: the liberated wheezing of Amy Beech's bagpipe concerto, when all of a sudden Lillian appeared, crouched on the lowest branch of a baobab tree. He was made up in black face, with whiskers. I was appalled since the Glyptic had spotted him and then spat knowingly in my direction. I asked him to leave at once, which he corrected into "vanish." I said for heaven's sake. He announced loudly that he was a spayed black Cheshire cat and would only consent to vanishing if asked to do so by a dashing, blue-eyed aviator. An aviator with old-fashioned earflaps he added with a smirk as the Glyptic drew closer. I looked over imploringly at Rod who was quite naked by now beside his radiator and surrounded by a gaggle of Beverleys; I knew he could not hear my call for help above their din. They were attempting to toss him into the air from a tarpaulin thing they were all holding. Or something. It looked to me like Miss Fake's poncho with the headhole sewn up. Anyway, I had to do something to divert one's attention from Lillian on his branch, and took the draconian measure of spilling tarts (strawberry and quince) on every lap within the drip line of the baobab tree. Olive O. got one in the face but she did not even blanch, accustomed as she is to viscosity. Even Velva got an unintentional one on her rose, the precious. I hurled several quinces at the Beverleys but they merrily smeared them on their thigh-high boots. What I'm saying is this: I failed somehow to distract attention from Lillian; in fact, I foolishly succeeded in making everyone look up at him since by this time he was the only untarted one at the whole Garden Party. Lillian loves an audience, and he began to show off his gartered ass (my garters I add in dejection) as he capered along a branch, smiling rudely, and singing the most ghastly lyrics (to the tune of "Jolly Good Fellow") about the sexual quirks of Chaucer, Dryden and Christopher Smart, which latter I question. I felt a little ill but in command. I had to pull in the reins smartly and knew it. I called out to Miss Fake Glyptic leering at my elbow, "You really should get your mother down and go home now. The party's over." Lillian, the dear, went right along with it, adding, "Only if Mumsy lets me take home her aviator boyfriend." Well, the Glyptic froze. Quite literally. We put her out with Old Oxe in the snow. She was even invested with Lord Oxthorpe's cigar before we all rode merrily home in sleighs and bells furnished by Frau McCarthy — nice gesture on her part with a curious condition attached to it, however: we must all arrive home *before midnight*. Isn't that quaint? One of the group, that wretched professor Silvio Bung, said he would have no truck with superstition and after depositing us all at our respective doors, he drove off never to be seen again. Velva claims she heard distinct clucking sounds emanating from his person just as she got out of the sleigh on the stroke of midnight, but I do doubt. Off.

December 3

This is going to be a *larmoyant* entry and may even be "detached" eventually. It all started when Velva discovered her pet terrapin had a galloping carcinoma. Prognosis: rotten. We redecorated the nursery where her pet held sway; I wrote several quick, clever articles for *The Toad* to pay for the chintz I ordered at considerable expense from Ireland. All this flurry for nought. Velva was inconsolable, and in her state of shock accused me of deliberately depressing her pet with all that cheap chintz. I let her rant; the poor dear was quite incoherent; she asked me why I wasn't a nun if I thought I was so smart, etc. Curious. The dark side of her Rose, I fear, has cast its shadow over all. Well, I was in a state of dejection and called up poor Tanya Scève for a consultation. She received me the same day (the third I believe) in her frigid little studio located above the Municipal Skating Rink. She insisted I remove my gloves so she could come into contact with my fingertips, which I thought excessive since she kept her own gloves on. Then, to the strains of the "Blue Danube" waltz coming from below, she circled me three times, in the fashion of a skater even though she was wearing what looked like membranes on her feet. Her eyes rolled into the back of her head, she became as stiff as Lot's wife, then slowly fell unconscious to the floor. I tried desperately to awaken her. I even struck her blue, strangely small face once or twice, but nothing. I finally left by the back door as she had instructed me to do over the phone in case of an emergency, but I confess I was in a dreadful state. I'll wager Frau McCarthy could have done better than that. It was a shameful abuse of the sensibilities. Not to mention my ass; the ice accumulated therein spent a week melting. I went home and did something I may regret: opened L.L.'s tome on medieval cookery and am now tempted to try his recipe for high cock. I think the reason may be the fact the text is written in iambic pentameter and when one is depressed, nothing soothes the heart more. Off.

December 3

Velva made terrapin soup the other day. I turned down her invitation to partake of the concoction even after she had insisted it was *mock* terrapin soup, shrieking with laughter the while. I think her grief has unhinged something. Gillespie was seen at the theatre wearing a vampire brooch. IT may be a female after all. I haven't checked the story (Velva was the source, and in her state . . .) but it sounds plausible. Anyway, it brought a ray of sunshine into my valley. Cannot seem to shake off the mists. I know what would cheer me up but Rod took my "fuck off" literally and has not popped in for days. But then he is so shy; he may be writing me a note right this moment with one of his unpublished poems quivering on the page . . .

As I write this, I can hear Lillian rummaging in the next room and it does unnerve. He told me he had been converted to Islam and needed a fez. Why he supposes any of my clothes might resemble a fez is unreasonable. I have no hats of any kind. Oh dear, I just heard a loud "*Eureka*" from the next room. Where will all of this lead? Off to investigate.

Later: The wretch! It's all too ghastly for words. Lillian has locked himself in my documentation closet and says he won't come out until I die. He also said he had found a fez, albeit crushed, and asked me who had forgotten it under the bed. He began screaming *Inch Allah* at the top of his lungs and I had to call the police.
Later-later: Frau McCarthy just called and asked if I ate fowl. I was naturally cautious and said, "High or low?" She hung up.

December 3

The Glyptic has just put out a pamphlet in which the creature flatulently states that the final solution to the

Québec problem lies in the construction of a tunnel between the Redpath and the University of Montréal libraries! She's done it now. She'll be back bending Ontario hairpins any day now and thanking her stars for
the job, too. Really. A tunnel between the libraries! Can
you imagine all the screwing that would go on down
there between the two solitudes? And all in franglais,
too. She's been terminally mad since birth although
lately she's been slipping faster than ever — that is, if
"slipping" can be applied to the act of falling from the
bottom of the pit. She has probably done more harm
with her pamphlet than all of Diderot's writings did for
the Revolution. By-the-by, speaking of Diderot and libraries, I hear L.L. has a monograph out on a heretofore
lost Diderot manuscript which turned up quaintly
enough in L.L.'s own basement library! In one of the
gutted refrigerators that he and his grandfather before
him used for storing notes apparently. The gall! I think
that he too has "slipped" these past years if you can call
"slipping" the act of falling from the bottom of the pit. I
hear the manuscript is a novel Diderot toyed with for
years in secret. In a foreword, he instructs posterity to
bring the novel up to date according to the morals of the
period. Spurge has leaked the title to *The Toad* which I
record for the record: *Creep, Nun, Creep.* If it had not
been L.L.'s "discovery" I would have had no hesitation
as a long-standing Diderot woman in publicly backing
the authentic ring the title has. Given the stench L.L.
calls his intellect, however, we can only remain tight-
nosed about the whole thing. I do wonder how he's go-

ing to update Diderot's morals though, even if the novel is a spurgery in the French *canular* tradition.

December 3

Lord Oxthorpe came by to tea with a bevy of boy lute players. He refers to them as his "angel peds." When I arched an eyebrow he explained that "ped" was a truncation of "piano pedal." All very transparent, and I must admit that Lillian has tutored my eye in that realm. It does seem so removed from the Greeks, though. I mean Old Oxe is no Socrates no matter how many *eromenoi* hang on his lips; does he realize this? Is it important? I even wondered whether I should serve them quinces with their tea and thus spark a polemic, but I resisted the temptation. A little too rude for a quiet afternoon. Anyway, I had to be prudent since Lillian is still locked in my documentation closet and insists on crowing loudly every hour on the hour. After a particularly shrill crow, one of Oxe's ruddy-faced luters asked me if he might inspect the cuckoo clock he had just heard in the next room. I told him it would be at his risk and peril since the clock in question was an old-fashioned cock clock. Old Oxe howled, "Lydia, you're a thigh slapper!" He became apoplectic and had to be patted on the back by several of the boys; the only words the old dear managed to sputter were, "Lower, boys, lower." God, I thought the whole thing would never end. But just then the boys broke out their lutes and began playing lustily. Their variations on a rococo air seemed to soothe away

Old Oxe's fit. He leaned back in the armchair he always brings along with him wherever he goes and remarked, "Lydia Thrippe, we salute you." Then he fell asleep and the boys instantly went through his pockets for loose change, piled their lutes on his lap and raced giggling from the room. This is what I mean about the distance from the Greeks. Shameful and sad. Even Lillian must have been moved because he forwent his hourly crow.

December 3

Went with soft Velva to Gigglehook yesterday to meet with Mrs. Waning whose claim to fame is her gardening gifts. Velva had told me she was brilliant — a Trollope woman — so naturally I was prepared to be on my intellectual toes. Well, her snow-heaped garden was something of a disappointment. She insisted on showing us around a perfectly bare expanse of flower beds, naming the plants which should have been there. Indeed, for Mrs. Waning I dare say they were there. Interspersed with her remarks on invisible plants were occasional asinine allusions to the non-existence of God and a reference to Leibniz's enduring popularity among thinking persons. You can imagine I pricked up my ears at this last enormity since it rang Spurge bells. I mentioned to Mrs. Waning that I knew a certain L.L. Spurge who shared her convictions and then the cat was out! It appears that she and Spurge are bosom buddies! I was not amused by Velva's little practical joke (she had known about all this from the beginning) but all she would say in her defence was that when one is at Gigglehook one must do as the Giggles do. I started away at once but before I could get far Mrs. Waning put an icy finger around my waist and dragged me over to another utterly barren bed; indeed, the snow was so deep there that Velva was up to her rose in it. Serves her right, too. Mrs. Waning informed me that in that bleak bed I was contemplating splendid specimens of *Euphorbia epithymoides*. This was the last straw: basically of course I'm a mycology woman but I have enough green botany under my belt to know that *Euphorbia epithymoides* is the common *spurge*. Hateful. I left Mrs. Waning on the spot and Velva as well who was asking in her boringly coy fashion what was growing in the next bed. Just as I hailed a cab I heard Mrs. Waning answer loudly for my benefit: "Why, as you can see, all the flowers that are growing in this bed are in pitiful shape. They have been invaded by insect pests, the most vicious of which of course is the common . . ." But here I knew what the old Snow Drift was about to say and I let out a shriek and pretended to faint, knowing Velva would come running. We did not speak a word all the way back to Upper Egg-Buckland. She must have experienced a slight twinge of conscience because she paid for the cab. I do not intend to forgive her lightly. One must keep one's priorities straight where hurt is concerned. Off.

December 3

The immovable date is an increasing annoyance. I'll have to devise a system to keep the thirds where they should be. I remember that last year at this time it was November for months. Ran into Rod's basket at Steinberg's yesterday. Quite by chance, but he seemed to think not. He said in an unkindly loud voice, "So you've tracked me down, eh Lydia Pinkerton?" It was so nice to see him again that I ignored the negative hypocorism and asked him if I had somehow damaged his basket. He threw back his head at this and bellowed, "Puke!" By now there was a small knot of customers with thick eyeglasses all around us. I tried to reason with the boy but he would have none of it, preferring instead to bang his head boringly against a shelf and cry. The scene later inspired a subtitle for one of my monographs on Julian of Norwich that I had been searching for for months: *Apollo Weeping*. It was both beautiful and frenzied: that Etruscan nose, that Adonis brow, the heels of Hermes and the body of Iupiter — all quivering in sorrow in the bathetic aisles of Steinberg's! It was too much for me; I took the darling by the arm and tried to lead him out of the store but was thwarted by a petty cashier who stopped us and insisted on inspecting our things: she barely glanced through my handbag but the silly thing spent much time going through Rod's personal effects, especially his pockets. Once outside, I reminded him (still blubbering) of his sweet folly of a few years back on a day of rain; of how dapper he had looked in his dissolving trousers: his only reaction was to try to bang his head against a parking meter but his aim was off. I finally got him into the elevator at my building and he said something about the virtue of elevators was their capacity to go up. I felt the old thrill dampen my femininity but he would not stop weeping. I gently pointed out to him that his performance today would provide a splendid title for a monograph but that I now had enough material and he could stop crying. I think the man struck me at this juncture but here the psyche-saving blur begins. All I do remember is Rod with froth on his face saying that orgasms are for birds and that his elevator wouldn't go upstairs anymore. I surely must have dreamt the last bit. Surely Rod . . . Oh, wait till I tell Velva when we are speaking again! Off!

December 3

Note from Mrs. Waning ordering me to read *The Perfect Garden at Gigglehook* and informing me she would send along a copy as soon as she published the book. She included a "recent" photograph of a snowdrift with the caption: To refresh your memory. She must have little to do but bait people. A trick she caught from the Spurge I expect. Hers is not the usual viciousness you associate with a *bas bleu*. There's a certain mannishness about hers which would have dried up Christina Rossetti's vapours for life.

Will be attending the Annual Book Fair to replenish my stock of acquaintances. I hear that Gillespie is at death's door. Vaginal decay it appears, so that settles that. Moreover, Miss Fake Glyptic is ill and I wish her as much.

December 3

What a lark! Went to a séance at Frau McCarthy's yesterday and it was a corker. One of the guests was Ramsey Bishop who wanted to know something about the future but would not say what it was. Frau McCarthy insisted he spell it out but he absolutely refused, saying his question would remain *in petto*, and if she was as good as her reputation would indicate, she should get on with it. There was also poor Tanya Scève who had come, she said, "For a few pointers." My God, the woman has a draft in her head instead of a mind — pointers, indeed. I can still see her after that shocking display of incompetence at her place, lying on the floor, stiff as a cod, and blowing bubbles through her nose which she had the gall to include later in her honorarium as "inchoate protoplasm." The nicest person there was dear Velva Rose who sat next to me. When it came time to touch fingers around the table, our little rift healed right over, leaving a scar perhaps but both patients doing well! Her smile, when our fingers melted together, was seraphically moist. Oh, I was about to forget: the Glyptic was there to find out whether her illness was fake or not. She looked as ghastly as unleavened dough; I was tempted to remark that she has been fake since birth, but my spirit was on higher planes. Well, to cut to the séance proper, the Frau demonstrated she is a professional: from her mouth there oozed an emanation in the shape of a foot. Then from some other orifice emerged another foot, rather pear-shaped. They were not attached to anything or to each other but instantly proceeded to tap dance round the table top. The Frau warned us not to break the finger chain even if the feet should happen to step on us. Then came a soft shoe number by one foot while the other seemed to be resting. The Frau, in appropriate sepulchral tones, asked the feet who they are (or were). There was a long moment while they remained eerily still, then from the toe regions there issued the following curiosity: "We are Diderot then and Diderot now." The Frau was delighted and asked them whither and whence. They answered that all the alleged wisdom and science contained in their Encyclopaedia was utter compost and should be used as such; that the Shadows on the Cave Wall are cast by the Ideal Tap Dancer; that the Prime Dancer, however, is long past his prime and shouldn't be dancing at all, and that Aquinas was an Ass; that the dance *qua* Dance feeds on its own *ness* and why shouldn't it. I couldn't help interrupting the feet at this point as Velva's hands in mine were getting moister and moister; I asked them perforce about *Creep, Nun, Creep.* It was obvious they were stunned, but they rallied at last to denounce the thing as a Spurgery just as I had suspected, and to declare that that man would be deprived of tap shoes when his turn to go on the Great Dance Floor should arrive, which punishment would continue until the frittering away of Sisyphus' rock should be accomplished. When, at that juncture, the Glyptic asked the feet about her illness, the ghostly pair promptly dissolved and nothing Frau McCarthy could do would bring them back. The Frau apologized but said it was not her fault; that the circle was damp somewhere along the line and a short-circuit had occurred. Ramsey Bishop was furious and said he had been foolish to consult a pair of feet without asking them first whether they were joined to a body politic or separate from it. Velva and I hurried out and tap-danced all the way home, like tipsy piglets in a fairy tale. Off.

December 3

Gave my last lecture at the University today for this term. Only hulking Oblomov was in attendance, playing with my lectern as I walked in. When I asked him where the other students were, he turned on his tape recorder, closed his moon eyes and ignored me. I hesitated for a moment since I had prepared a somewhat dramatic lecture to round off the year; my working title was *Mummy Fungus from Seven Egyptian Tombs and its Link to the Isis Cult*. It had taken some research and I felt reluctant to waste it all on a tape machine. After a moment of indecision, however, I launched into the thing, spreading out my notes carefully as is my wont. Twenty minutes later as I was building to the climax I pounded the lectern firmly to make my point and to prepare my audience for the finale but to my horror the support gave way and my notes flew about the amphitheatre. Oblomov let out a scream, raced out only to come back instantly with the whole class who had been waiting outside. A glance at the lectern showed me the support had been sawed quasi-through and that it was all a trap. I very sharply informed my students that their antics were not indicative of graduate thinking; that their sally was actually a rape of the Comic Muse; and that if they did not wipe the smirks off their faces I would fail every last one of them. The last remark triggered silence: they all filed to their seats and sat down with open notebooks. Alas, my notes were at the four cardinal points and I was in no mood to improvise. I told them in loud tones, looking straight into Oblomov's moon eyes, that their crime deserved punishment which in this instance would consist in not ever knowing how Isis fitted into Osiris. They sighed (I think), closed their notebooks noisily and thought it cute to cancan their way to the exit. Oblomov remained behind, still seated and seemingly absorbed in something he was writing. I stalked regally past him, glanced down at his notebook and was most gratified to see he was doodling *spores*. I had won! Off.

December 3

Just returned from Gillespie's funeral. The pallbearers were four alarmingly small midgets who had their tiny hands full, believe me. I caught a glimpse of the Glyptic looking like unleavened dough even through her veil.

She was also wearing an apron that the creature had obviously forgotten to remove. Over her coat at that!

Rod popped up as words were being uttered at the grave side. Apparently he had been lurking in the cemetery before we arrived because he seemed quite surprised to see us there. We were all called upon to admire the series of igloos he was building among the graves which, he said, he had gone to great pains to render authentic. I extended a well-gloved hand to him but he turned his back on me and crept into the smallest igloo whence the whole funeral party could hear him weeping as the ceremony continued. Well, they lowered old Gillespie into the earth "to return to Its atoms" as I said once in a poem of youth dedicated to my pet lark that departed before its time, taking childhood innocence with it, alas. Oh yes, and then the very round priest at the grave side slipped and fell, and "the fat was in the friar" as Velva, the soft darling, whispered inconsistently at my elbow. To lift the priest out of the pit took all the pallbearers, the sexton, and Rod who was prevailed upon to leave off eating chocolate baby seal eyes and help. When that skirmish was over, the priest discovered he had lost his breviary and his cruets. Since he was quite drunk, he decided to improvise and poor old Gillespie got the wedding ceremony, the only thing the old fool could remember, as exit line. I felt a little sad since I bore no grudge, just curiosity. The matter of the footwear still intrigues me . . . My reveries were interrupted by a singular act of molestation: Lillian, all in leather dressed and smelling of my best perfume, roared up on a motorcycle and kept gunning the thing as we stood there by the grave. I wondered fleetingly whether I had time to get back home and change the locks on my doors — on my documentation closet door in particular — but Lillian was motorized and probably knew what I was thinking. He had that *air* about him. He also looked younger than ever with quite a jaunty tilt to his persona; I just don't know where it will all lead. It was at that moment that the gravediggers threw down their spades and refused to cover poor Gillespie; apparently their union had declared a strike was to start just then. There was nothing to do but to lug the coffin up again and put it back into the hearse. I hear they put the body into a refrigerated *chapelle ardente* where it is to remain until the strike blows over. The small pallbearers were furious of course at having to do the whole thing over again in reverse order. Just goes to show you that you can't even count on a hole anymore to swallow you up.

I must read something elegiac in anapests. At once.

December 3

At last attended a proper social function which dignity attended as well: the Annual Book Exhibit inaugurated by Her Majesty, the Queen. She had come at the behest of the *guhvuhmunt* to help hold this country together. I can say the policy is working because not one of the troublemakers in this province attended. All was serenity and English. When it came time for the Queen to cut the inaugural ribbon, a small chicken on a leash strolled by and stopped Her Majesty in mid-snip; she frowned faintly and her security people scooped up the bird and traced its leash back to Frau McCarthy who was then bundled out. After this little *contretemps*, the ceremony went ahead as planned: the ribbon fell away into two clean parts and the Queen said, "My husband and I sincerely hope the symbolism of this gesture will not be lost on your great country." Lord Oxthorpe boomed out, "Hear, hear!" The Queen produced a radiant smile, so everyone shouted, "Hear, hear!" When the smile vanished because Her Majesty could not unclasp her handbag, her security people instantly gave her another one, identical to the first, and the smile returned. It was all very moving. A reception line formed as we were to be presented to Her Majesty. This was a surprise! No one had been told beforehand; apparently it was a direct order from the Queen at the last minute. I don't know how the Glyptic got to be at the head of the line, but there she was, looking like unleavened dough, her whole body racked by gale force trembles. The Queen extended her free hand to Miss Fake who rudely fainted on the spot. The security people scooped her up and bundled her out, her body still twitching like a galvanized frog's leg. Trust the creature to strike a gross note! Actually her faint was a blessing since I had heard via the vine that she had intended to expose to the Queen her tunnel idea linking the two solitudes. Can you imagine . . . When my turn came, the Queen asked me about my latest publication. She seemed very well informed about my work although she did confuse my name and L.L.'s. I gently corrected her, mentioning the fact that L.L.'s latest thing in print was a hoax. Her Majesty seemed delighted — for diplomatic reasons I have no doubt — and asked me to draw a moral. I must say I was taken aback: I could find no link between *Creep, Nun, Creep* and a moral of any kind. I confess I flushed and begged to be excused. The Queen frowned and naturally tried to open her handbag, again without success. After the security people had given her another bag, she smiled and passed on to shake hands with Dom Paddy. He was grotesque in a sort of Friar Tuck outfit. The Queen addressed him as Dom Tuck, which I thought was brilliant; Dom Paddy swallowed several times and said he had not had the pleasure of being introduced to her . . . There was an awkward moment while the Queen tried vainly to open her handbag, etc. Dom Paddy expressed interest in the Queen's tiara and asked her if it had been properly blessed. The Queen graciously replied that it had been fashioned from the oldest garter in England, having once been worn by Edward III himself, although not in its present location on her person. There was a murmur of awe at this, and Her Majesty passed on as Dom Paddy made uncouth blessing gestures behind her back. I leaned closer to him and stopped his nonsense with a sharply whispered, *"Lèse-majesté*, you ass." He leaned over to me and said something in Latin which I won't repeat. Straight out of Krafft-Ebing it was. Luckily our polyglot Majesty was out of earshot; she was now talking to that Marjoram Kelp woman. She was wearing a dress of messy seaweed that had extensions right up through her hair, terminating in a conch. The Queen, beautifully briefed, asked her about her sea plants mounted in glue, and the Kelp reeled with delight. She had the indecency, however, to press a straggle of fresh kelp into the Queen's radiant glove. Happily, the handbag opened this time and the weed disappeared in a twinkling. I spotted Mrs. Waning near the end of the line, looking stiff in a gown shaped like a dirty icicle; and at the very end of the line was vulgar Minerva Mount, one of Velva's former acquaintances. Whatever Velva saw of interest in the creature is a mystery. When the Queen approached her, she sank down into a curtsey so absurdly low she could not rise to her feet. She struggled there on the floor as Her Majesty fumbled in her bag. At last the security people scooped up the vulgar mass and bundled it out. The Queen made another charming speech in which the clarity of her thinking was matched only by her complexion. She expressed satisfaction at having had her deepest convictions about this country confirmed by the cross section of persons she had had the occasion to examine today. She rounded off her little talk with a gracious wave of her bag and a remark about never forgetting what it all means in terms of the whole. Then she left and the guests thronged around the book tables. I posted myself behind my table and was ready to sign copies. Well, the rush was on! It was only half an hour later, when I finally had a respite from my fans, that I realized with horror someone had switched tables on me and I had been autographing copies of the Holy Bible. I looked up to see L.L. holding a handkerchief to his eyes and rumbling with laughter. Without further ado, and in as tasteful a fashion possible, I set his handkerchief on fire. He had to be hospitalized, but the best part is that everyone there saw his toupee go up in flames. That should dry up his fountain of youth or I'm not Lydia Thrippe. Even Mrs. Waning pressed a cold finger around my waist and whispered, "Congratulations." Coming from her the remark carried some substance if little warmth. I rejoiced and looked around for Velva to hug. She was nowhere in sight. I learned later, with no small emotion, from wretched Dom Paddy that the Queen had refused to attend the Premier's sugaring off party on the grounds that enough is enough, and that she had invited Velva and the Glyptic to a *thé dansant*. More of all this later, as I have just had a rush of envy which I must discipline at once by reading a page of Dryden. Off.

Later: To complete this entry that started out on such a jocund note and has now edged into low drama:

Item: the chicken Frau McCarthy had with her is her *natural*, that is her psychic link to the Unknown, and as such never leaves her side. I suppose this explains something.

Item: towards the end of the book signing, Dom Paddy came up to me and said he was puzzled by my uneconomical use of so many *begats* in the first chapter of my book. I struck him.

Item: the invitation to the dancing tea by the Queen and which supposedly included Velva and Miss

Fake was all a hoax. What actually occurred was a sur-reptitious meeting between Velva and Minerva Mount. I seethed when I learned this, and try as I might I cannot control myself. I shall try the variorum Dryden this time but I have my doubts. Lord Oxthorpe with his court of angel peds may have the solution after all. Velva and Minerva Mount! What a bad dream life is to be sure. Off.

December 3

Séance yesterday at poor Tanya Scève's. I made two things very clear to her before accepting her invitation: one, no repeat of the Lot's wife act; and two, Velva Rose was not to attend. I gave no explanation for the second condition but the firmness of my *timbre* brooked no twaddle. I noticed with relief that her studio seemed warmer than the previous time and that the Blue Da-nube waltz was not booming up from the skating rink below. The reason, according to our hostess, was be-cause when it is husband and wife night as it was then, no music is played since it was a waste of time and money. Poor Tanya Scève can be a cynic at times but she is seldom convincing. I've noticed these occasions usu-ally coincide with her being in the company of intellec-tuals where she hopes her cynicism will pass for bril-liance. Poor dupe I say, but you can't talk to adults anymore. The other guests included Lord Oxthorpe who said he had had his armchair reupholstered for the event (now, there's cynicism for you!); Olive O., whom

I have seldom seen away from a clutch of males, and I must say she did have a little lost waif air about her; the fourth guest, to my discomfiture, was Mrs. Waning. I think I would have preferred even the Glyptic to her since we all would rather bear those ills we have than fly to others etc. When it came time to make the finger chain around the table, Mrs. Waning clamped an icicle index finger around my wrist, promptly turning it blue. I felt the cold seeping into my very teeth but fortunately poor Tanya Scève noticed my plight and kindly deployed an electric tablecloth. After a minute or so my wrist was still a little numb but we could proceed. The lights were dimmed and a knocking was heard at once. When asked who the knock was, it replied: "The ghost of Gillespie of course." Consternation. Even Mrs. Waning made a queer gargle sound while Old Oxe's borborygme was deafening. After a few moments poor indecisive Tanya Scève still did not know whether she should dismiss the spirit and if so, how; finally Old Oxe said he had a question. There was an awkward hush. Then:

"Since you are dead and buried it can't hurt to tell us what your gender was in life, now can it?"

The question had naturally been on all our minds, but Oxe must be truly obsessed to have found the nerve to talk of sex to the dead. The Knock replied that all that would be gone into at the proper time but for the present Gillespie was indeed dead but not buried. Even after the gravediggers' strike was over, Gillespie's aunt had refused to permit the body to be deposited in the family vault because too little room was left: Gillespie being inordinately broad, there would be no space for the aunt if her body were allowed therein. But, continued the Knock, there were a few accounts to settle *en attendant* which would pass the time until Gillespie was buried. It asked where I was and Mrs. Waning coldly and promptly denounced my location. At once I felt a sharp rap on my fingers but I could do nothing to protect them. "And that," said the Knock in a tone of grave re-proof, "is for your unkind thoughts about my foot-wear." I started to marvel at the meanness of spirit of even the dead, but cancelled the thought just in time. One more rap and my writer's wrist would have devel-oped a severe case of carpal tunnel syndrome. Olive O. was rapped next for having spread endless rumours about there being a sealed void between Gillespie's legs. I had not heard that one but then we do move in differ-ent circles — usually. Mrs. Waning got a hearty rap I am pleased to report because she had diffused a ghastly story to the effect that what was really between Gillespie's legs was a buffer zone between the two known genders. Only Lord Oxthorpe, who has always taken a great interest in the sexual orifices without prejudice either way, escaped the wrath of the Knock. He very gently said, "Tell us, dear departed Gillespie, what had you/had you not there where the bee sucks." The injection of the poetic note did the trick, because we could hear weeping and the saddest of voices that said:

"I was . . . (tears and gnashings) . . . I was . . . (high wailing like that produced by Arab women in the presence of a corpse) . . . I was . . . a . . . homeovestite." Consternation. Only Old Oxe nodded knowingly and told the rest of us he would explain later. He instructed Gillespie to rest in peace and reminded us all that consolation should be sought in the fact that the shroud fits all genders with equity and love. As Gillespie sobbed in relief, Oxe explained to us that in life Gillespie had been either a woman dressed as a woman but with the profound conviction she was a man dressed as a woman — or the inverse. The whole thing, from this standpoint, was most illuminating. I am now reviewing my acquaintances with some trepidation. I wish I could talk about it to Velva but certainly not while vulgar Minerva Mount is under her roof. Just had a thought: will send a Christmas card to Velva in my best uncials and will hint that there may be less to Minerva Mount than meets the eye — or *more*. Off!

June 22

The calendar change I have been through is pleasant indeed. Much froth has passed under the bridge but the bridge is still there. Some things will not change: I have it on good authority that the Glyptic wears a corrective stocking on her right leg. To what end, one wonders. One also wonders what the silly thing is correcting. Could it be to attract attention to her limbs? Not likely, since she has no legs as it were, rectified or otherwise. It certainly bears out Blake's pithy comment to the effect that "Secrecy gains females loud applause." But a corrective stocking! What could she be correcting? A tattoo from the heady, reckless days of youth? Titillating but ultimately cheap.

June 22

Spurge plucked three hairs rapidly but not painlessly from my forearm yesterday at the annual Day of the Dead luncheon (very late this year). My rancour was real; any contact with him is odious to me; the feel of his fingernail was moilish in the extreme and his use of my first name made me stiffen: "Lydia," said he, "this is the day of the dead so we cannot be too careful. We must think of ultimates now or never. These three hairs may be all that's left of your brilliance when death has taken a husband's leave of you." I suppose I should simply have punched him and let it go at that but I felt I had to answer: "If fingernails and hairs were all we're about, how do you account for saints and poets? We all worry about the body's image too much, including the dead body's, but I ask you to tell me if the borthens growing on Keats' corpse were rooted in the soul?" Well, that stopped the wretch in mid-metaphysics and as he dropped my three hairs in disbelief, I snatched them up and tucked them where no man goes. To finish him off before he could rally, I proposed a toast with great gusto: "Drink life to the lees and have faith that the Ultimate Enema will come on little cat feet when no one is around to see us except our Solitude." L.L. fell strangely silent and began fumbling in his fly for something. Off.

June 22

The Reverend Wasperd de Winter narrowed his eyes at his congregation from the height of the pulpit last Sunday (this from Velva as I don't practice) and informed them he suspected one of his parishioners was a *mole*. He expanded on this to say that the mole had been probably planted in his parish as a tot at the font and had grown up spying on his archontate. A thigh slapper! Velva even hinted to me that *she* might be the mole in question, which is so soft, so sweet. But then she can never leave well enough alone, adding she was an *unconscious* mole whose mission had long been obsolete. She even suggested that she has had intimations of certain past experiences that could only have come to her from another and loftier life. It was then I realized the darling thought the Reverend was talking about a mole who had been parachuted into his parish from heaven. I'm afraid I did little to discourage her fantasy: her eyes became so attractively damp as she confided in me! Off.

June 22

Finally have received an explanation for the inexplicable: poor Tanya Scève was recently in communication again with dear departed Gillespie (now that she's been properly inhumed, the epithets are flying again: "old gap legs"; "old gap-toothed vagina," etc.) and after much prodding of plasma Gillespie talked *d'outre tombe* about her atrocious footwear. It would appear — although poor Tanya Scève's stories have more warp than woof anymore — that Gillespie was a closet freak, in the sense that she was a freak about closets, i.e. *water closets*. I do remember those huge green letters W C sewn on her sweaters but I was led to believe (this from Dom Paddy) that it stood for *Weird Cunt*. But I digress. The footwear was atrocious only by female standards apparently, for whenever Gillespie had a "male seizure" she would don a sturdy orange pair of boots which promptly made *her* into a *him*, then would go to a certain Water Closet in the suburbs in order to display the footwear to the others sitting in their stalls. Evidently the competition is fierce; a veritable fashion parade of stout boots, vigorous sneakers and moody moccasins. These are admired or disdained from every angle, and whoever has the most virile foot is elected best cobbled man and is then fêted. No details were transmitted to me about the fête proper but from Dom Paddy's Latin, I gather it harks back to the most primitive of rites, involving reliable Eleusinian things like the contemplation of corncobs, etc. I wonder whether Lord Oxthorpe knows this little vignette? Which reminds me I must record something juicy about Old Oxe, but not today. My face hurts. Off.

April 11

They keep tampering with the dates, the years, and my face. Why even bother recording so-called "exact" days? All is illusion.

47

The Glyptic has just returned from the Holy Land (her way of mouthing "Holy Land" is obscene) with what she claims is a piece of the True Cross that she bought on the black market. Her corrective stocking must be strangling more than just her leg. Oxygen must be cut off at the pass, as it were. She also claims to have come across, in a bat-filled cave, an old Semitic remedy for her unleavened dough complexion. I record all this drivel because Velva (the source of course) wants me to remind her of it all in a year's time . . .

I have absolutely nothing to say today except to wonder aloud at the fathomless crassness of certain people. The Glyptic brought back a little souvenir from her journey for Velva: a clay pelican *sans* beak. Even soft, polite Velva was a little stunned, and when she gently pointed out to the Glyptic that the bird's beak was missing, the Glyptic retorted haughtily, "Well, you've got most of the bird, now haven't you?"

March, for heaven's sake

I discovered by chance that Dom Paddy, who had disappeared after burning down the seminary last Easter Sunday, has set up a consultation booth near the waterworks which he refers to as his "small sanctuary." The police have raided it several times but he seems to have connections in Wootton Wawen where the booth is located. I sought him out (after some hesitation) for advice on a hatefully ambiguous — and likely defective — ablative absolute in Krafft-Ebing. He seemed genuinely pleased to see me but it's hard to tell, what with the permanent smirk he sports on all occasions. After giving me the only stool in his exiguous quarters, he served me an evil-smelling toddy he claimed to have made from scratch, called Essence of Gilead. It turned my head — and stomach — but I did not let on. We chatted about this priest and that nun and why some saints are more fashionable than others until numbness set in. I detected a new and most annoying habit he has developed: instead of the papal *we* he was wont to use, he now prefers the haughty third person singular! Just to show you: after my query about Krafft-Ebing, linguistic chaos ensued: "We certainly don't want him to tell him about his relations with them." (*We* = himself and me I think; first *him* = himself I presume; second *him* = Krafft-Ebing?; *his* = Dom Paddy? Krafft-Ebing?; *them* = priests? nuns? ablative absolutes?) All very tedious. By the time he got to the ablative absolute proper, he was singing old Latin ditties like *Qui legit non peccat* for starters. They ranged from Caesar's light, scabrous verses (I was ignorant of the fact that the Latins had metal mattresses and therefore onomatopoeia) to variations on a rude graffito on one of Browne's urns. I accused him of sophomoric sciamachy, which made him pull in his drunken horn for a moment or two. He then went for another bottle he claimed came straight from the cellars of the Vatican, the herbs fermenting therein having been gathered by one of the Borgias on the eve of his election to the papacy. I think the man wanted me to leave, or faint, or challenge his facts, but I tossed down the concoction immediately. The female has much more alcohol tolerance than men suspect or than what we let be known . . . Dom Paddy very solemnly emptied his goblet, leaned forward and pronounced the following rudity: "He isn't going to tell you about absolutes, whether ablative or wablative. He says he knows everyone, especially you, calls him Paddy Waddy behind his back but that is his punishment for having pushed those cute adolescents into the hot-cross bun oven —" He broke off his lucubrations to try to embrace my leg; I managed to free it as discreetly as possible, only to find the other one in his damp, sticky grip. "Dom Paddy," I said loudly and with not a semiquaver in my voice, "I can understand your excitation: it is due to the economy of the Latin line. But your reading of Krafft-Ebing has unhinged the devil in you. Tell him to get behind you." Dom Paddy's smirk extended into his hairline and he retorted, "Not on your life. He likes it there, you know." I could see he was raving and that I would have to put my free foot down. I began to describe my latest book in exquisite detail, omitting nothing, and before long his eyes glazed, his grip came unglued and his whole body fell with a dull crack to the tile floor.

As I drove home to Upper Egg-Buckland, I reviewed the events I had just lived through but no amount of analysis would throw any sane light on Dom Paddy's behaviour. Was he mad after all? Just drunk? Merely *exalted* perhaps . . .

Some of my friends wonder what I see in Velva; but after the shocking display of skewed thought I witnessed this afternoon, surely it is essential that one occasionally embrace wholesome ignorance, furry thinking, and above all the bald mind. Off to work on my new monograph on Pepys; working title: *The Mirror as Manuscript*.

April again

The crocuses on my front lawn are being buried under artificial snow at this very minute by Herr Klapp, the aggressive heel-clicker who lives next door. Every year at this time he takes umbrage at the temerity of early spring flowers. Armed with a wheelbarrow full of snow-machine snow he goes up and down the street burying every living thing that pokes itself out of the cold earth and grumbling as he does so, "Stupid crocuses, stupid snowdrops, stupid, stupid tulips," etc. He is standing at attention out there right now, saluting the mound of ice he has shovelled on to my poor crocuses. I heard his heels click together a few minutes ago and it reminded me of Dr. Silvio Bung's remark to the effect that heel-clickers are suffering from a masturbation fantasy and that they actually want to knock their knees together but, for practical physical reasons, have lowered their libido to the heel. (Bung is a specialist on the heel but a piker compared to Dom Paddy). The explanation is not entirely satisfactory; one has only to glimpse Frau Klapp to realize the woman strongly suggests the aggressive insecurity of an Irish washerwoman.

Later: I went out to tell Herr Klapp to click off my lawn and leave my plants in peace. He saluted smartly, snapped his boots together and stared hard at me as his trousers slithered slowly down to his heels. A complex man . . .

Later-later: I must refrain from jumping to hasty conclusions as I did about Herr Klapp earlier today. I've decided after reflection that there is more to Herr Klapp than meets the naked eye. More later perhaps. Off.

April still

Là-Là, my French-Canadian niece, produced a new doll for my inspection the other day at her parents' table. It was a loathsome little thing with plastic soap suds for hair and a biodegradable face. She unscrewed the head and filled the cavity with ketchup, then screwed it back on, humming atonally as she did so. Her parents (one of whom is *not* Lillian) claim she is very clever but I can't judge: she never speaks when I'm in the room except to shriek, "Help!" whenever I smile at her. I was vexed when her mother unctuously stated that Là-Là had my brains but her father's brawn. But to proceed: Là-Là put the doll on the table, pumped one of its arms thereby forcing it to emit a hooting noise, then tipped the thing up and removed a napkin placed on its bottom. The napkin was stained with ketchup and Là-Là screamed in delight. Her mother and father paid not the slightest attention to her nor to my gagging. I left before dessert, pleading a headache. It was only when I was home, un-dressed and bare, that I discovered the little beast had managed to hide the napkin in my purse. The reign of King Stephen comes to mind when it was reported that "Christ slept, and *His saints with Him.*"

April still

As I was skimming through *The Fecalized Heel* the other night, I was increasingly aghast at Dom Paddy's travesty of scholarship. In this book he has undermined not only the foundations of psychoanalysis, but damaged (I sus-pect irreparably) his mind. The burrowing that goes on! The frantic scratching as tits and tattles are heaped in ant-like desperation! The scurry of nervous claws in every sentence! (Look what he's done to my otherwise sober style! Exclamation points the way some people have mice!). I wonder what Herr Klapp's reaction would be if I slipped it under his door . . . I imagine it should throw his heel-clicking off centre for a time, or it may transfer his habit to his pet parrot. The thing spends its waking hours swinging on a crescent phallus for perch, and screaming at the passers-by: "Hi Ying! Hi Yang!" Dom Paddy says in his epigraph to *The Fecalized Heel*:

"There is a confusion in most minds between *ying* and *yang*, *yoni* and *woni*, *whump* and *thump*, and of course most commonly *six* and *nine*." There is a whole chapter where he expands on this drivel, and why I read through it is a mystery. Perhaps it's because of the gaping hole it leaves as it burrows through one's psyche. The overall impression when you put the book down is something akin to what a runner must feel who has suddenly and inexplicably become splayfooted and knock-kneed. Anyway, I am not going to review his book for *The Toad* since he will be odious to me whether I do or don't. What I might do is write an anonymous note telling him a rival has written an exhaustive treatise on the fecalization of exclamation marks and their place within the pleasure principle. It's worth a try even if he spends the rest of his life shaking his head and murmuring, "Can such things be?"

Early July

Summoned by Mrs. Waning to tea. I could have refused of course but bygones should be. Nor, as is my wont, did I ask her who would be present but accepted at once. I think she was a little taken aback at my prompt decision. Keep them off guard, I say. The Reverend Wasperd de Winter called almost as soon as I had hung up the phone to offer me his "wheels." Silly ass, adding that he too would be among the guests at Mrs. Waning's. Had he been on another phone while I was talking to her? How could he have known so soon I was going? Had he perhaps overheard the whole thing from a vantage point in another room at Mrs. Waning's? It was my turn to be taken aback, but I did tell him I would be delighted to go with him *and* Mrs. de Winter. There was a pause, with much crepitation on the line, followed by this curiosity:

"After de Winter, can de Spring be far behind?" Then dead air— or so I thought. I said in French, "Imbécile" into the mouthpiece and immediately heard a soft, "*Et tu, Brute*." Really . . . Well, I called my Velva to ask about all that; she told me there has never been a Mrs. de Winter; that as a young seminarian de Winter had had a memorable *dry dream* so impossible to ever approximate in the waking life that he swore himself to celibacy for the rest of his days (and nights).

The Reverend picked me up at half past four and we sped to Gigglehook in silence. He was wearing an old slouch hat for no apparent reason and was perspiring profusely. His clerical collar was limp and I could have sworn that vapours were rising from the whole sartorial mess. I wanted to ask him about that adolescent dream of his but thought better of it— what if it were apocryphal? I wondered too about the potency of that long-ago dream: had it been just a metaphor, an analogy, an allegory, or something quite rude? I'll save the question for a garden party and those dreadful lulls.

Mrs. Waning feigned ignorance of my identity at her door. The Reverend introduced us as new acquaintances and she opened her eyes very wide on hearing my name as though my presence were quite unexpected. She had caught me off guard once before but I vowed she would not do so again. I thrust out my hand, wondering if her body temperature had risen with the summer solstice, but she let her wrist hang stiffly as though it had a cramp, and that was an end to *that*.

Many slences later we sat down to tarts and tea. Mrs. Waning made not the slightest effort to stimulate anyone's mind, merely groping in the folds of her dress to no obvious end or staring sullenly at her cat. She poured one or two drops of tea for us, barely covering the bottom of the cup, and literally threw a frozen tart on our butter plates. The Reverend was jolly throughout all this rudeness, commending Mrs. Waning on her exciting use of vervaine instead of hyson. I toyed with the tart but it was quite hopelessly solid, with ice-crystals winking at the rim. When de Winter asked if the tarts were to be conserved until next Christmas as a special treat (he said this with a laugh, mind), Mrs. Waning looked away in gloom at her cat and said, "Blessèd are the fools for the coma they create in others." The Reverend laughed much too heartily, then slipped absurdly out of character by pounding his chest with delight. Mrs. Waning glared at him, rose noisily in a fuss of chiffon and left us alone in the room. Even de Winter was a little unnerved but turned gamely to me and said, "What are your views, Miss Thrippe, on the coma?" I mentioned de Quincey's use of the word in a comical passage of the *Eater* where a fly falls into a coma because he comes too close to a drunkard's bad breath, but the Reverend did not appear to be attending.

He was staring past my left shoulder at something that obviously had him spellbound. I turned slowly to see Mrs. Waning seated in front of an easel in her garden, busily painting and laughing the while. I mentioned I was unaware that Mrs. Waning painted, but by now the Reverend had risen to his feet, still holding his tea-cup. He then walked stiffly out the french windows and into the garden. I watched him stare numbly down at Mrs. Waning's canvas which I, from my disadvantage point, could not see. The Reverend suddenly grew pale and trembled enough to make his forelock tumble all over his brow. Surely even a bad painting of daisies and roses, I mused, could not induce a look of such pure horror on his face. My curiosity got the better of me and nearly tripping over the cat, I went into the garden to examine the painting. Now, the climax to this entry has not been created lightly, nor *ex nihilo* just for the effect it will undoubtedly produce; no, it is the truth, unblinking: amidst the blooms and hues of her July garden, Mrs. Waning was busily painting a view of the same garden under several feet of snow! At the top of the canvas near a mound of off-white cones and drifts, she had scrawled the following title: "De Winter." No wonder the Reverend was in a coma. Even he could find no levity in this affront and taking my arm, he led me from the spot with a whispered, "Come Lydia, I dislike scenes of any kind, especially painted ones."

December 3

Back to basics! My favourite date has come round again, like the old gyre it is.

Went to a play written, produced and staged by the Glyptic. I was dragged there by Lord Oxthorpe whose latest buzz is promoting, at great expense, little experimental plays with boys only in the cast, his sole condition being their age must not exceed thirteen. Well, this play was about an octogenarian dying of tertiary syphilis who was the object of much cruelty from his two grandchildren, all three actors of course being not a day over twelve years of age. Really . . . From the program notes one learns the Glyptic's message is that novelists have lied to us about love; that youth loves as badly as it does everything else; that only age knows what loving is. But then why depict the Octo as being deaf and mute? Sign and eye language on stage can become tedious very quickly. The action, therefore, consisted mainly in thumpings on the Octo's back, punchings and kickings and battery of every description accompanied by much giggling from the grandchildren who, it appears, were having an incestuous love affair, albeit a bungled one. The Octo had a cat (a little, stuffed, vicious-looking sock) which he insisted on rocking in his arms violently, dribbling all the while. The climax came when after a very nasty beating of the old man in the best bastinado fashion (the Glyptic should have simply made a catalogue of torture tactics), he proceeded to disembowel the sock. He then put it over his head, covering his eyes; the point of all this, announced on a sign that was carried across the stage by a boy wearing a sandwich board and nothing else, was to show that love is deaf, dumb and blind. After the curtain had crept agonizingly down, there were a few dull reports from the poor trapped audience, and someone whom Oxe had paid handsomely got up (he was all of eleven) and screamed in an endearing castrato falsetto: "Author, author!" The worst was yet to come: a spotlight searched and *found* the Glyptic, simpering and blubbering at the rear of the theatre. Old Oxe stood up, applauding and dragging me to my feet. Once the Glyptic was on her feet and the fake humility had gone, she promptly made an hour-long speech on the love-wish motif that informs Hebrew thought. I positively reeled in rage for she had plucked the main idea from my youthful treatise on *"Muhammad, Man or Mountain?"* Had not dear Oxe held on to my shoulders I should have collapsed then and there. As it was, I stood bravely through it all, biting my lip and singing to myself. The actors, whom everyone had forgotten about, fell asleep on the stage while the eight-year-old pianist (who had accompanied the play as though it were a silent film which it was not) slid from his stool and crept down the aisle until he was beside Old Oxe and myself. Thereupon the little darling lifted his leg, doggy-fashion, and peed firmly on Old Oxe's tux trousers. Umbrage was briefly taken (just for the gallery) but when Oxe saw I was all wreathèd smiles, he nodded to the tot and beckoned him to stand up. The boy stood on tiptoe, kissed Oxe's belt buckle and Oxe melted. He picked him up, placed him on his shoulder Saint Christopher and Christ child fashion; the three of us waited numbly until the Glyptic finally sat down, wiping her eyes and snuffling the while.

We all retired to a discreet Vietnamese restaurant afterwards where the dishes were ordered by Lord

Oxthorpe in impeccably fluent Cantonese. Delightful postlude to a disaster. During the pork dish the Glyptic stuck out her tongue at me when no one else was watching, but the gods were on my side: she was unaware that her tongue was coated with a rude, gelatinous lacque that gave her the appearance of an ineffectual gargoyle. Off!*

---

* This is the end of the *Diary* but not quite the end of Lydia. Other than the "detached leaves" there is a bundle of manuscripts and documents under seal for charity's sake. I plan to publish a selection from them fifty years hence. I have tried to keep order in the above extracts, limiting my choice to the more uplifting passages. In keeping with Lydia's own intention, I shall publish what is left over as "detached leaves" which, as the Thrippe herself states elsewhere: "No writer worth her salt would not leave behind for posterity to mull over, a collection of detached leaves." I have, therefore, every intention of doing this for her. One of the last things she said to me before silence set in was, "Look to my detached leaves, Sloate, and let the chips roll where they may."**

** *One* (emphasis mine) of the last things she said, and indeed she thought it necessary to proceed with an explanation of her fusion of *chips* and *roll* as a final bow to her mentor, Mallarmé.

The Lydiad

A series of manuscripts carelessly lost in various places (monks' sandals, freight elevators, spineless books). The series has neither head nor coccyx but that is all right too, since it is addressed to no one, in particular.

The footnotes are unnecessary and tedious, as indeed one would expect. It is not clear why they were appended, but someone must have thought them necessary.

But, then, even Maeterlinck weakened and wrote a long footnote called The Life of the Bee, *or words to that effect.*

Victoria, or The Shameless Toes

Victoria had a father, a mother, a house, a bed, a doll, food and drink, a cat, the proper number of playmates, a book of pictures, a room of her own and an elongated ambition to become a heroine. One day her toes began growing shamelessly. She lost her doll, her cat, her playmates and just about everything else. Her mother died of embarrassment and her father could no longer stomach her. She was refused food and water on the theory her diet was to blame and she was put on a strict regimen of hymns, copybook headings and air. To no avail. Her toes turned to sausages and made frying noises in the night. When her father's head gave out she was locked away where she ultimately became a heroine in a wallpaper. Her shadow remained fixed on the frivolous pattern of leafy things on the asylum walls long after she had died. Her rakish uncle on her father's side had her toes pickled in brine and as far as anyone knows they are on his mantel still, inappropriately labelled: *Victorian Toes.*

Leonard, or The House that Cracked

Leonard bought a cracking house for no sensible reason. A clue might lie in the fact that he had once collected baby trotters and his mother had a list and thus walked oddly. His playmates had always unravelled his socks in the normal, cheery way deviants have, so this is not much help. Delving deeper one comes across a naked hare in his background (and his bed) that nobody ever explained satisfactorily. And Leonard defiantly brushed aside all probes into the lobster claw he had found in a men's room, as he proceeded to explore all the fissures he had bought with his daughter's money. The one who had died without a trace only days before May Teck vanished. Some of the cracks would have to wait for his old age, so deep, so deep. Others would not keep crooked and suggested paralysis. The one he liked best was as wide as the Grand Canyon and was called "Doro-

thy" for the sole reason Leonard could call it "Dot" in
the middle of the night and laugh sickeningly to himself
until dawn.[1]

Mother Teck, or The Unavowable Nuns

Mother Teck bought a used convent. There were only
two nuns left in the building; they had vowed something
which Mother Teck's mission in life it became to find
out. They lived in the cellar right under Mother Teck's
cell. One (as far as Mother Teck could guess) slept per-
pendicular to the other, thus forming a human cross.
(Mother Teck never found out whether they did this naked or not). All she could see in her morning rounds
were the dustless parts of their cell, shaped like a T. Was
silence one of their vows? They would not tell. Was one
of the vows sleeping nude in the form of a cross? Was it
perhaps not a cross but a T? Did the T (if it was one)
stand for anything? How many vows had they taken?
They both pressed their noses against the wall, as mute
as the stones. Mother Teck had one last question: If they
were nuns (Mother Teck was not even certain of this)
what was their Order? Their habits were so chewed and
tattered that Mother Teck could not identify them to
save her soul. No answer forthcame and the years
passed. When at last, spent and old, Mother Teck went
down to the cellar to beg them to tell her their vows before she died — or at least, in charity's name, to tell her
how *many* vows there were, she found they had not
been sleeping in the cellar for years. They were up in the

attic, sorting through their endless collection of irregular sulphur cubes.[2]

Alphonse, or The Marvellous Leg

Alphonse lost his leg in a manhole in Surrey, England. The artificial limb he ordered was a marvel: it had nine joints so it could move in any direction: other than up, down, forward and backward, it could also go sideways, lengthen or shorten at will, inflate and deflate, buckle or stiffen, spin and pivot, cake-walk and sing a song. There was a stipulation in Alphonse's will stating his nephew should have it, and cherish it, and keep it waxed and oiled. His nephew, Alphonse the Second, was properly disgusted, but he took the marvellous leg home with him anyway. In time he grew quite fond of it (it would sing him to sleep, nights) and he took to taking it everywhere with him in an old cello case. He began losing his closest friends (the leg *would* sing hymns at parties in gloomy, and because it was inside the cello case, *hollow* tones). Actually, Alphonse the Second did not regret the loss of his friends after he discovered a mouth, cleverly concealed, in one of the leg's joints. They became truly inseparable and loved to spend their Sunday mornings in protracted romps. Ecstasy reigned until Alphonse the Second got the unkind idea of putting it in the oven for twenty minutes, then slipping it under the covers of his bed in the guise of a warming pan. The leg was not amused and slowly ate him to death. Its explanation at the Southampton Customs Sheds was that it needed "substance" for its long voyage home. The Customs Officer directed it to the "British Subjects Only" file, and it sang its way to Surrey, where it had never been, but thought it knew the place because Alphonse the Second had talked of it often when explaining its Family Tree. The marvellous leg wrote a long and learned article on its trip,[3] giving a list of all British manholes in Surrey and a number of stars like the Michelin Guide to each one, depending on its holiness. Years later, long after the leg had been laid to rest, it was discovered that the old cello case was in reality a case for a *viola da gamba*. Could this have been an accident? Did Alphonse the Second know? Did the leg know, and choose to ignore it? The enigma lingers to this day, or at least, variations on it.

Carey, or The Wages of Greed

Carey cut off a finger when she was three. This infantile mutilation was analysed by parents, doctors and nuns. The only explanation of the bizarre incident the little patient herself would give was this excerpt from a manuscript Lydia Thrippe found years later stuffed into a shoe box: "I thought it was jam or jelly, I forget which." No amount of analysis could cast the slightest ray of sense on her childhood amputation. "Pure depredation!" shouted her mother to the walls every noon as she drank her first scotch of the day. "Jesus!" her father would say through dentifrice foam as he did his teeth in the morning. As she got older, Carey noticed that more and more persons of note came to see her and the precious space where her childish finger had been. "If they come in droves to see one absent finger," she reasoned, "what would happen if I cut off all of them?" She did just that. When the curious came to tea next time and found her utterly fingerless, they were disgusted and ignored all her invitations thereafter. In desperation she cut off her toes, her elbow-angles and her kneecaps. To no avail. Her charisma had vanished; that magic, pristine Space had expanded to vulgar Infinity. Carey died a very disillusioned, mephitic old woman, albeit streamlined.[4]

Trudy, or The Secret Aphid

Trudy had a crotch beautiful. Largely well-proportioned except for the head, which was really a convex, inside-out navel. This he duly contemplated from dawn till star-rise. Then others did. He had a small ant for pet which he kept in an old-fashioned toothpaste tube. He likened his destiny to a ship's and the ant's to a captain's. Which is to say (other than the obvious) that Trudy's sense of balance was erotic in the extreme. The ant would graze upon his face, ear and nose hairs then work slowly down to Trudy's rudder. This he would stroke, fondle, manipulate and steer as though it were an aphid until the juices flowed. So passed the nights and the years. When Trudy's crotch beautiful went to pot, the ant did not seem to care. Oh, it rubbed its hind legs together more often, perhaps, when alone, but youth will out. By-the-bye, this is a happy tale as I have omnisciently decided and therefore it will now end.[5]

Lolly, or Ars Celare Artem

Lolly was a mechanical doll, *à la Hoffmann*. She belonged to a rather big girl also called Lolly. Her mother, to distinguish doll from girl (like two peas in a cliché except for the rococo key in the doll's bum), had their dresses made so their asses always showed. Whenever the slightest doubt stabbed Mother, she would simply wheel the girl (or the doll) around quickly to reassure herself. The key was the key. Over the years Mother grew nervous however and took to chewing sideways on her hair bun since her daughter stubbornly refused to grow any older than her doll, whose age for all eternity was ten. Lolly-*girl* made other people nervous for sundry reasons: her white hair betrayed her real age (in her late fifties); her cheeks were as pink as a ten-year-old's; her dresses were terribly out of fashion and too snug; her ass showed quaintly whenever she left the room.

Only one man ever attempted to cross the line separating girl from doll, but he retreated when he ended up with a hand full of key. Mother was rather pleased with the whole arrangement, but selfishly died before Lolly-*girl*, which precipitated a tragedy: Lolly-*doll's* springs finally rusted right through and since Lolly-*girl* was too feeble to protest (she was in her early nineties by then), they buried Lolly-*doll* in the family plot. When it was time for Lolly-*girl* to migrate, they mistook her for Lolly-*doll* and threw her on the city dump. The mayor, in a tiny ceremony, announced that her private parts were now public property, and that one and all might rummage through her insides because (a sly wink at this point to the small audience of rats) "there must be a pretty good thermostat somewhere in there to keep an old girl like that going so long."[6]

Tante Pute, or The Others

Tante Pute was a laid-off madam who had used up three thousand two hundred and two lipsticks in her career. She was very proud of this, well, let's say the word: sexploit, and had kept each tube which she displayed in her basement playroom on hand-tatted rugs. She searched through the want-ads daily but laid-off madams were in great supply and the demand was nil. Tante Pute started a crusade which can be summed up thus: "Why were so many perfectly reusable madams destitute?" This was the question she painted (in lipstick characters) on banners, on sundry toilet walls, on her panties (alas, now a little frayed around the holes), and on city sidewalks. An old priest who lived in a drum finally revealed to her that madams were superfluous henceforth and that their functions had been usurped by Others. "What Others?" screamed Tante Pute. But on this point, and invoking professional and confessional discretion, the priest was mum. Where to turn? Usurped? Impossible. How usurp the plyers of the Oldest Profession? Might as well usurp the Universe! Or drink all the Milky Way! What Others? Tante Pute saw red. She put an ad in the papers and offered her collection of empty lipstick tubes in exchange for information leading to the identity of the Others. Months passed. Then an anonymous telephone call told her where to deposit her collection; the information she sought would be at the same place. Imagine, dear Reader, Tante Pute's confusion when, lugging her full trunks of empty tubes, she found she was at the gates of Paradise! There was a crawly sort of inscription over the portals in sticky red characters which read:

Your crack has been metamorphosed into a lipstick tube.

A small but profoundly nasty arrow was pointing at Tante Pute's Tube with a sign saying "Males Only," thus smoothly integrating her nicely for all eternity.[7]

Tormada, or The Ball Crisis

Tormada was a converted Spaniard and hated every minute of it. He had written to a mail-order house and was sent The Spanish Kit for next to *nada*. It seemed a bargain: one gallon of near-virgin olive oil, pointed, high-heeled shoes, a sombrero, two slightly damaged banderillas, a guitar, three hairs of the Poet forming the initials F.G.L., a tiny windmill, a long-playing record giving instructions on how to acquire a genuine castilian lisp, and finally two rubber castanets. Tormada was enchanted with his Spanish Kit at first. He would put up his longish hair with a mother-of-pearl comb, put on his shiny ankle boots and heel-dance, toss his sombrero high in the air and wait for admiration. None came. Usually, as he clattered his way down Main Street, there hung the heaviest of silences. All chatter ceased; children stopped fighting, plotting and urinating. Only once did Tormada hear a voice whisper into a moonlit shell-shaped ear on a perfect romantic night under a shady doorway: "He must have small balls." Tormada puzzled over the remark for years, exploiting every possibility of his Kit, even putting on a free recital of old favourites played on the rubber castanets. Indifference. Except for the same voice once again whispering, years later, into the same shell-shaped ear: "*Tiny* balls, I'll bet." So Tormada started hating things Spanish and disenchantment set in. He shed his fineries. Off went the sombrero skimming over a green pond with pink ducks; the near-virgin olive oil was poured over everything else in his Kit, thus making a salad for the townsfolk. Everyone came to the feast, eating everything but the rubber castanets which, they insisted, Tormada should keep to cover up his small balls. In total fact he was now naked, and for the life of his sanity he could not remember his original nationality. What had he been before opening that Spanish Kit? No one would tell (or knew) (or cared) but they did put their heads together and composed an epic poem which, until recently, was chanted by children and crones in doorways:

Tormada had too[8] smalls[9]
Too[10] tiny to be balls[11]
He doffed[12] his cloths[13]
But took no baths
So by all he was shunnèd[14]
His smell everyone stunnèd[15]
He was playing by the shore
With a leprous whore[16]
Counting rubbers[17] and bores[18]
When sod —[19]

Vivuums, or The Crux

Vivuums is an essence. She comes in every dimension, not the least of which is love. Her mechanics are erotic dynamics; her stasis is a porno frieze; the parts of her whole are scattered on every eye, reassembled at a tug upon the mind's zipper. Vivuums is lambent softness, malleable perfection, pneumatic humidity, in short the faceless Organ. Vivuums is always at hand, always open to all, only a wish away from wet warmth. Her migrations are infinite: totally present in the autistic fist of the adolescent or the beautiful wedge come between bored lovers. Her vanishing act is total and clean, banished by a muscular spasm. Today Vivuums is waiting as usual to be called into brief existence by a mind somewhere. Let us not forget, however, that her Male Counter Part now exists: the delight of women and perverts and whose name is unpronounceable. And He is *seeking her out.* Will He and Vivuums meet? This has become the ulti-mate, cosmic organon in all philosophies, all metaphys-

ics, most toilet walls and all crotcheries. Miss Lydia
Thrippe, librarian and amateur mycologist, has written
a paper entitled *The Crux* hypothesizing an eventual
meeting between Vivuums and the Unpronounceable
One. After the usual brilliant dialectical pyrotechnics,
Miss Thrippe's conclusion is uncharacteristically bold
and lacking in her well-known academic reserve: she
formally maintains that such a meeting has to occur if
masturbation is ever to be curbed. A curious, nearly illegible footnote makes mention of an immediate and
cosmic increase in the world suicide rate but apparently
the statement will have to wait for another paper by
L.Thrippe for expansion.[20]

Polly, or/and Paul

Polly was secretly a man in woman's panties. Her/his
parents had decided on female issue and when Polly appeared wearing the usual male accoutrements, her/his
parents put their collective ids together and simply ignored Polly's addenda. Polly was raised Polly: bouncy
ringlets until twelve years of age and bangs afterwards
well into the pubic years. Masturbation, triggered by
Polly's furtive readings *à la flashlight* under midnight
blankets, was accomplished by means of an adroit finger
introduced under the prepuce and twirled widdershins.
The white results were long mistaken for the menstrual
flow and Polly dutifully masturbated once every
twenty-eight days, even though she/he found the time
long between periods. Exposure of course was inevita-

ble: it happened on Halloween which also happened to be her/his wedding night. Polly's partner (we shall call him Paul for ambiguity's sake) had refrained from the usual fumblings before their nuptials and so they were quite unprepared for whatever occurred. Reports are conflicting. Actually, as far as Lydia Thrippe can ascertain (this from a footnote on a new enzyme she discovered in the *Amanita virosa* which proves conclusively that most deaths are psychosomatic) Polly was unmasked as Paul, and Paul, once his pants were down thoroughly, was basically a Polly, although the footnote breaks off here in mid-ecstasy. No one seems to know anything at all about the actual goings-in and-out of that night (Miss Thrippe's footnote, alas, may even be apocryphal). All we *do* know, and this merely adds to the confusion, but we feel it should go into the dossier anyway, is that Paul and Polly opened a Diner outside an automobile plant in Windsor Mews, Ont. The diner was a remodelled handcar.

Little Arley, or l'Être et le Néant

Little Arley was a dead baby. He had been breathing our air for only a few months when his soother dissolved, filling his tiny lungs with rubber. Little Arley was given precious exequies with potted cypresses and a converted jewel box mounted on pink casters and drawn by four black-plumed ponies which served him in the office of a coffin. It was most effective, bringing tears and chokes to everyone except his brothers and sisters. Little Arley's

parents were properly inconsolable. They totally ne-
glected their other children, and lived only for their
dead baby. Little Arley would come back at the oddest
times: whenever one of the living children broke things,
the parents would evoke Little Arley's pacific nature;
whenever the living children were caught playing titty
winks, it was slapped into their minds via the bum that
Little Arley had lived and died without fooling around;
that Little Arley's baby fixtures had gone back whence
they had come, unsullied, unfingered and in a word,
precious. Needless to say the living children grew to
loathe little dead Arley. The parents prayed daily for his
second coming and because they were good at it, their
prayers were answered. Unfortunately the other children found him first, lying in his little cradle that had remained enshrined in a nursery annex, and promptly
smothered him beneath his precious brocade pillow. A
sumptuous funeral followed, with the now familiar evo-
cations about Little Arley's goodness in all things, both
liminal and sub. These incidents recurred at least several
times — Lydia Thrippe states flatly that Little Arley had
come on five separate occasions although L.L. Spurge,
ichthyologist and amateur mid-husband, disagrees but
refuses to say why — until the living children left home
when age allowed and started the whole process over
again. Which somehow explains Little Arley's alcohol-
ism somewhere, somewhat.

Treadfoot, or The Cosmetic Self

Treadfoot woke up one morning with an excression. The specialist told him not to worry since it was obsolete. Had it been a *growth,* however, room for disquietude would have been ample. Treadfoot was thrilled with his good fortune: his Mums had always informed him in her lucid fits (somehow included in her major work entitled *Glass Anomalies in the Sands of the Sudan*) that he was born too early. His obvious counterargument was invalidated by the specialist's declaration that if he was still treading Earth's gypsite paths it was thanks to a hapstroke: his extra cock was a delightful obsolescence and therefore impertinent. Treadfoot's Mums was fascinated by the justification of her convictions about his born-ness, buttressed by the physical evidence at hand, which she fondled with objectivity (it was obsolete, she would say). Later, she demonstrated in another article on Sudan sand folia that certain sand roses had similar obsolete shapes. Miss Lydia Thrippe has not replied in the Occidental reviews.[21] Treadfoot himself drunkenly compares his twin cockery (one resolutely contemporary, 'tother totally archaic) to The Adam on the Sistine ceiling. All of which doggedly proves once again that one turns unflaggingly to the Authoress of one's days for cosmetic insights into one's own intrinsic box.

Grimthorpe, or The God-dabbler

Grimthorpe was an aggressive pedant. All specialisations were his province. He was once called upon to restore a cathedral (in his expert architect stage); he transformed it instantly into a five-hundred seat outhouse without even really trying. It was a masterpiece for anyone who had an eye for outhouses. Grimthorpe had.

One was painted around each hole, making the vacuum the pupil; the iris was a rainbow of pastel *putti* and lofty whims. In his expert couturière phase (with perforce the alias Maggy Prespot) Grimthorpe introduced codpieces for women, quaintly sheathing the breasts, all ribbony and things. It was his master contribution to the unisex fad but it faded after Lebanon fell to the Irish. In Grimthorpe's painter phase, old masters were made like new with true grimthorpian touches: cough drops were put preciously, but not quite congealed, in all of Rubens's anuses, the fusion of drop and flesh hailed as a Gorgian touch that left the critics gagging. But the Virgin of the Rocks with real rocks for tits was considered his mastergag. Grimthorpe the linguist duly transformed English into a target language, shooting it full of holes and quoting the Swiss Saussage as reference (later repudiated as indigestible). As sociologist Grimthorpe waved his magic mind and changed Marx into a collective agreement that stipulated Sunday was a Chicken to be eaten Every Day, the condition being that all Gentlemen Farmers take their shoes off and walk upon cowshit the way everybody else did. And Grimthorpe the criminologist was a marvel: the victim miraculously became the criminal in 100% of the cases he examined. His paper entitled *The Willing House* showed in superb detail how sick homes really are, leaving their doors agape like lubricious laps. Even the rape of Miss Lydia Thrippe, librarian and martyr, was shrugged off as an exception, the only witnesses being discredited by Grimthorpe when he noted they all wore rings in their noses. But Grimthorpe the psychoanalyst was the apotheosis. All other phases paled beside his perfect grasp of human, botanic and crustacean psyches, and the brilliant proposals he put forth to fix their fissures. His first step was to have all patients, human or botanic or crustacean, sign a confession dictated loudly by Grimthorpe to the effect they had sexual problems, incurable and hopeless. The second step was the inspired guess that made his reputation: he declared himself God in Gothic script on jaconat parchment and copies were given to all sickies and most mothers over fifty. Grimthorpe now tends bar in a teen club because, as he says as he mixes air and words, "God the First had a Son who came down Here and Farted around. Why not Me?" This gauntlet has not yet been picked up but not so Grimthorpe himself who allows his person to be, and incessantly, world without end, but means galore. Amen for now.

Haboob, or The Wind Gatherer

Haboob was an avid wind collector. He had boxes, trunks, drawers and rooms full of wind which he had gathered, in his travels, at each cardinal point. From the East he brought back, in a well-wrought wind glass, the blithe airs of a gentle creature who used to stand tiptoe on Arabian dunes in the moonlight. Her whispered phonemes of undying fealty were scooped from the sand by Haboob when her attention wandered to his navel, and placed in immortal storage. One remembers that all wind gatherers must collect their tenuous effluvia when the collectee is unaware or dead. From the West Haboob's trophy had a case of proxy: he bought, from a habnab wind dealer, a small quantity of gas reputed to have been expelled by Socrates only minutes before expiring. Haboob promptly transvased the paralysed scent from its original brass vulgar vessel into the most delicate of phart phials, wrought in obsidian upon a fairy chain and which he entrusted afterwards to the sole circumference of his neck and nothing else. From the North there was a belch that Haboob brought back from a Wood Pig whom he had mistaken for a Wood Lover after drinking half the Northern Lights during a xylophone orgy in a Lumber Camp. Haboob kept this one in his cellar among other North things, none of which he was particularly proud. From the South, however, came the airy jewel of Haboob's booty: the sweet vacuum trapped in the tightest runt[22] he could find. The possessor wanted to remain anonymous so Haboob will carry its identity to his grave, of course. There is another long paper by L.L. Spurge, mid-husband and phonologist, in which he advances the amusing, if implausible, theory that the last gas mentioned issued instead from a trapped transvestite. The argument is floozy and is based on the propensity Haboob has always shown for catachreses, and that which was truly transvased, therefore, was the transvestite gas, not Socrates' at all. There is room, however.

West Forking, or A Regulation of No Consequence

West Forking was not a person. Nor a place. He was, for a change, an owl. Not one of your stuffed owls. West Forking was alive once and very round into the bargain, in body and eye. He was neither symbol nor simile. He resisted all attempts at allegory. His favourite perch was a makeshift phallus he had found on a night of rain, thunder and whumps. He had mistaken it for a dead mouse in the moonlight, only discovering his mistake once home in bed, with his cigar lit. West Forking installed the thing in the staff room where his colleagues tore things. Naturally a stand had to be built at considerable expense to accommodate it, since West Forking insisted on thermal-sensitive marble. Thereinto the makeshift phallus was inserted, with sufficient inchage projecting for West Forking to perch on. He *was* a sight; his colleagues loudly admired the whole setup but there was some envy in the airs under doors as Time passed.

West Forking took little notice, merely ruffling his feathers and looking ever so much like Johann Sebastian Bach at his organ. In his Memoirs there is much mention of this phase of his career but none of his colleagues remember it in the slightest. Indeed, they recall absolutely nothing since Death now absorbs their interest entirely. West Forking sat out many a generation in the staff room, looking more and more like a wig until the day someone put paint on his beak and talons. It was unkind, since old West Forking's eyesight had grown dim and the paint used was mouse-grey. He appears to have first eaten his talons, then proceeded to pounce upon his beak until the Dean intervened and quoted a longish regulation to soothe everyone exposed to the grisly ordeal. Later, West Forking was nailed to the staff room door like a flattened merkin where he is to this day if the moths haven't got him. Old West Forking! An owl with Heart! We all miss him and still wonder whatever happened to his makeshift phallus. It vanished on a night of rain, thunder and whumps. Without a trace this time, as the Archives, which vanished circa the same epoch, insist.[23]

Marjoram, or Our Lady of the Tarts

Marjoram was, and is, and ever shall be, of succulent gender. She gets into stews, adds dimension to your salmon, is at the bottom of many sauces and is interchangeable with the lowly earwig. The last is not true but Marjoram rolls her eyes ambiguously whenever you mention it. She possesses an accent which escapes geo-physical analysis but whose gender is impeccable. She speaks only in uncials, with illuminated eyeballs for starters. We have often been to her parties and wonder if others have. We talk mostly of "herbs" and "sea-weeds," gently but thoroughly corrected into "kelp" or, *à la rigueur* "sea plants." Marjoram is not a crustacean as you might think, but actually possesses a concealed bone which keeps her erect most of the time. She *is* a study! Her eccentricities are obsolete and leave one dormant, until with lugubrious grace she serves you one of her garlic tarts. Legend has it that Marjoram was once married to a Barber but we discount this as being a corruption of Berber. She has pots from that *liaison* which she and her husband wrought together, using the same wheel but different clays. The result is curiously disastrous, with a straggle of seaweed and/or kelp running through a pork motif. Her husband insisted on your cursive kelp pattern but Marjoram stuck to your green uncial: when the two collided, a child was born with stars, Wise Men and Metalinguistics all intertwined in flatulent rococo. Marjoram gives few parties now; her spouse ran off with a naked nun; her pastries are dull, made as they are from last year's recycled newspapers; her pâtés, once the talk of the toilets, no longer go to seed when bitten into; her feet, once sturdily corned, have turned to undependable mold. Marjoram! When shall we all meet again? Life is a dream, to be sure: you who were once the crust of the town! But we have not forgotten, and as we raise our broken glasses to toast the

Marjoram that was, you can hear a rumbling in the stomach that will never be fathomed. Three toasts for Marjoram, the succulent speckle on your trout![24]

Ratfurter, or Everything Your Rabbit Can Do To a Hill

Ratfurter was a literary concoction of L.L. Spurge, probably consisting of ground cardamom seeds, dangling gristle and loose ends. Spurge was brilliant at public relations (Miss Thrippe concedes this point but thinks it is mindless), promoting your Ratfurter where others durst not tread. He proceeded to convert the Jews, the Irish, the CBC, all academics and a German folk singer in leather shorts. All became rabid fanatics of the Ratfurter, following the thing over deserts, into ocean grottos, up volcanoes, down continental shelves, through and after male choruses, onto abruptly-emptied daises, across bed crumbs, toward shrill female oratrixes, around abandoned ponies at fairs, within Swann Lake remembered, behind Latin teachers on vacation, against rules and frigulations, along grasping cucumber vines for heavens' sake, amid implausible ovations, beneath overwrought linguists who had lost their theories, and finally betwixt and between all the above. Luckily Spurge had another cardamom up his sleeve since L.Thrippe (the Thrippe, as Spurge is wont to call her) was preparing a scather on the whole tedious travesty. When her monograph appeared, Spurge, forewarned, bought up every copy of the periodical and promptly recycled the paper. He wrapped your Ratfurter in the pages thus palimpsested, giving each one a preposition for identification, viz: the *into*furter, the *midst*furter, the *over*furter, the athwartfurter, etc. When the Thrippe learned of this infamy she orally informed her closest supporters that her paper had nothing at all to do with Ratfurters. "Actually," explained Lydia Thrippe as she archly warmed to her subject, "my article was on the abuse of treacle in Victorian England and was entitled *Gung-de-bah*."

Peg'ole, or The Wages of Paper Power

Ms. Peg'ole filed fantods from nine to five. She was directly under her superior and she often enjoyed it there. The fantods came in all flavours and one was even *spumone*. Miss Bagg, an innocent bystander, took ten and was reduced to vomit on the spot. Ms. Peg'ole filed away the mess under "Mousemother" where it is to this day. Our purpose here is to show what happens to persons in power: Ms. Peg'ole's superior was L.L. Spurge, promoted as he had been to head-handler. His nature had always been tenebrous, but his promotion made it corruptly opaque. He had ever been overly fond of paper even as a tot, but now he made paper tunnels and paper mazes and paper antimacassars the way he used to make paper Pipers, the sole aim of said tunnels, mazes and antimacassars being to confuse all underlings. This occurred with paralysing regularity and Spurge would promptly produce another fantod, which Ms. Peg'ole filed in a room to that effect, which in turn and in time became a department, which soon became a building with silos attached for unmanageable fantods that had suffered tears. As indicated above, Ms. Peg'ole was content under Spurge, this state usually taking place after the cottage cheese and watercress and before the greengages. So filed the years. One colourful remark in passing, however: Spruge was shot at by an old pensioner who apparently took him for a charging herd of paper. The sex of the pensioner has not been determined but we do know the pensioner has a degree in bibliotherapy. This is perplexing but can be filed correctly if one puts one's mind in to it.

Twenty, or The Article That Wasn't

There should be one last text here to make an even Twenty. But there just isn't. A few scribbles in Latin and fewer in Greek do exist, but have been ignored until further research does something. Spurge? The Thrippe? Well, as far as we know, yes. But whatever became of your old-fashioned scholarship? Where are the dependable, cast-iron index cards? Alas. Ultimately, it is this fart-gathering by old women in empty lots that makes us all whimper.

In any case, we wish everyone a Merry Life before Death, something Contained in every Container (on Sundays at least); and, of course, both sides of every Coin.

Lastly, and this is vital: End of the *Lydiad*.[25]

Notes

1. This text is actually a footnote to something else. It is signed L.L. Spurge.
2. Lydia Thrippe reserves judgment, but then she usually does.
3. The article is the unmistakeable work of Lydia Thrippe, arch and precious at the same time.
4. The ms found in the shoebox was entitled *My Mother and I*. The signature is truncated.
5. The "I" is not identified.
6. Lydia Thrippe refers to this text as "pure Spurge" and leaves it at that.
7. Text by L.L. Spurge and which I include to demonstrate the truth of Lydia's assertion that Spurge does to females what a rabbit can do to a hill.
8. Intentional levity. The poem has come down to us in corrupt form in the best oral tradition. We are using the only known holocene manuscript found in a monk's sandal and addressed to Lydia Thrippe, librarian.
9. The substantivized plural adjective is justified here since the fragment of the poem we possess is a transposition from the original Spanish, where this practice, abhorrent to the English ear, is common.
10. No Spanish surprises here.
11. Approximation. Original is untranslatable.
12. Slight evalution of language level for no apparent reason. One is reminded of passages in Homer where the listing of the names of ships and horses degenerates into doggerel.
13. *Cloths* and not *clothes*. Error?
14. Definitely a stressed "e." Error?
15. Notice stressed ultimate syllable. Segment defective in cadence.
16. One should avoid certain folklorish pronunciations of the word to preserve the rhyme. This is particularly true if one lives in Windsor-les-bains, hamlet located in southern Ontario, Canada.

17. No explanation given in terms of suggested multiple casta-nets. One presumes the two protagonists could count past two. Obscure reference to the loaves and fishes miracle? Error?

18. Perfectly gratuitous in the attempt here to form a rhyming couplet at any cost. Less than satisfactory.

19. The ms breaks off here in mid-word. The rest of the poem is alas! lost forever one fears. The mystery of "sod" has titil-lated more than one scholar. Suggested possibilities culled from hapless doctoral candidates who gave up on the thing: *Sodom, suddenly, sod* (as an entity), *Sudan sodden, sudamen, etc.* Most scholars concur with past and present researchers that the "s" is a certainty, but doubt casts its shadow on the "o" ("u"?) and the "d." Could be a "p." If so, the vista of variations is extended vertiginously. There is cautious room for hope, however: Lydia Thrippe is to publish a paper on the subject incessantly.

20. Lydia Thrippe has failed to comply. One can only surmise the whole thing is a *canular* which Lydia corked before it got out of hand.

21. That we are aware of at any rate. Her silence bodes ill for any quackery that might be involved.

22. Typo?

23. West Forking may be, after all is said and done, a faubourg of Windsor Mews, Ont., which invalidates everything. One is tempted not to jump to conclusions, however, and to give ovations when ovations are due.

24. L.L. Spurge delivered this text as a speech. The occasion has not been recorded.

25. The author of this article is in some dispute. We, however, are aware of the author's identity even if the author is not.

26. Daniel Sloate, bosom friend of L.Thrippe and a nodding ac-quaintance of L.L. Spurge, was persuaded to compile these texts since no one else would. He is responsible for annotat-ing and bowdlerizing Thrippe's Diary; the experience was so toxic he felt he could tackle anything. He has suffered the fate of the impartial scholar, however: Lydia and L.L. are not speaking to him or to each other or to precious few others. It's one of the sad truths of the Groves: remove the veils

from the face of Truth at your risk and peril. There are homes, however, for damaged scholars, and Sloate has applied for admission. We wish him well, all things considered. Of course the perky reader is now wondering who compiled the compiler. Alas, the information died with the computer it fatally infected. A note of caution: apparently the virus thus generated can be ingested by the mere act of reading the preceding texts. Antidote? Hardly. Goodbye.

Printed in March 1999 by

in Longueuil, Quebec